Shaun the Sheep™ MOVIE
SHEAR MADNESS

CANDLEWICK
ENTERTAINMENT

First U.S. edition 2015

ISBN 978-0-7636-7737-4

15 16 17 18 19 20 QGT 10 9 8 7 6 5 4 3 2 1

Printed in Taunton, MA, U.S.A.

This book was typeset in Manticore.
The illustrations were created digitally.

Candlewick Entertainment
An imprint of
Candlewick Press
99 Dover Street
Somerville, Massachusetts 02144

www.candlewick.com

CONTENTS

Chapter One

WHAT'S THE BUZZ?

Shaun the Sheep hated haircuts.

On shearing day at Mossy Bottom
Farm, all the sheep were led to a
small holding pen. Bitzer kept
blowing his whistle . . . loudly.
Shaun stuck his hoof into it to stop
the noise.

The Farmer walked into the crowded pen and turned on his shears. *Bzzzzzz!* The sheep jumped back, alarmed.

So, who would be first? The Farmer reached into the pile of sheep . . . and pulled out Shaun! He was going to get sheared whether he liked it or not.

The Farmer held Shaun tight around his middle. *Bzzz! Bzzz! Bzzz!* The job was done in two seconds flat.

Shaun heard laughter behind him. The Mossy Bottom pigs were leaning

against the fence. They snorted with
wicked glee and pointed at Shaun's
new haircut.

All Shaun could do was glare at
the Farmer.

The next day, Shaun had a plan. The sheep would take a day off!

First, the Flock needed to trick the Farmer. They moved the scarecrow to a spot behind the hedge. When the Farmer walked by, Shaun flicked a folded piece of paper at his head.

Hey! The Farmer looked at the sheep, who pointed at the scarecrow. Then they ran.

They didn't get far. The Farmer managed to stop them and led them back toward the pen. The Farmer counted the sheep as they jumped.

He didn't know that they kept
sneaking around to the other side.
The Flock jumped the gate over and
over again. The Farmer kept
counting, and as he did, he became
very, very sleepy. . . .

The sheep used a wheelbarrow to
carry the sleeping Farmer to the old
camper. Their plan was to make the
camper look like the
Farmer's bedroom. If the
Farmer woke up, he
would think it was
nighttime and go back to sleep!

The plan was working! The Flock
went back to the farmhouse to watch
DVDs and eat pizza . . . but not for

long. When Bitzer burst through the
door, their day off was cut short.

Chapter Two

THE CAMPER CATASTROPHE

The disappointed Flock led Bitzer to the camper so that he could wake the Farmer and get him back to work.

Bitzer tried to open the door, but it was stuck. He pulled hard. The camper rocked back and forth. There was a small log keeping the wheels in place, and the rocking crushed it.

When Bitzer pulled harder, the door handle broke off!

Then the whole thing started rolling. Inside, the Farmer was still snoring away. The camper rolled across the field and onto the road — toward the city!

Bitzer tried to hold on to the camper's bumper, but he lost his grip and fell in the mud. *Splat!* He got up and ran after the camper.

The Flock watched the camper — and the dog — in shock.

No Farmer or Bitzer at Mossy Bottom Farm? What should they do?

Get on with their day off! Bitzer and the Farmer would surely be back soon.

But the Flock couldn't get back into the farmhouse. The pigs had taken over and were having a party. No sheep allowed.

The sheep looked at one another sadly. Movie time was over.

And now, without the Farmer, how would they get food?

Meanwhile, Bitzer was still running after the camper. He ran mile after mile. That old camper could really roll!

Then, just as he reached the top of a hill, Bitzer saw something.

Down below, the camper had stopped, and the Farmer was being put into the back of an ambulance.

Bitzer ran toward them, but he was not fast enough. The ambulance pulled away and drove off.

Chapter Three

A NEW JOB

At the hospital, the Farmer was confused. Who was he? Where was he?

The accident had caused the Farmer to lose his memory. He did not remember Bitzer or Shaun or the Flock or Mossy Bottom Farm. He did not even know his own name!

The doctors wrote the name "Mr. X" on his medical chart.

The doctors showed the Farmer a series of cards to jog his memory. Was he a businessman? No.

A firefigher? No.

A judge? No.

A farmer? . . . No.

The doctors left the Farmer's room, but then another man walked in. He unrolled a selection of tools onto the bed and lifted a large hammer. The Farmer was terrified—what kinds of test needed a hammer?

The Farmer jumped from his bed and ran into the hall. The man with the hammer tapped a nail into the wall. He was not a doctor. He was there to hang a picture.

The confused Farmer ran out of the hospital and onto the city streets. But where could he go?

The Farmer wandered around, but still nothing looked familiar. Shops and storefronts blurred together, but then something stood out . . . a hair salon! There was something about those electric clippers. . . .

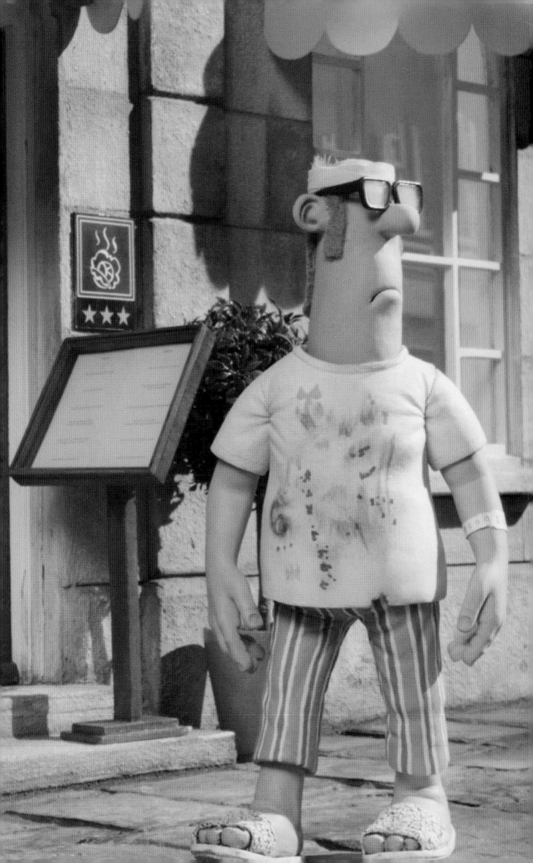

Suddenly a fancy car pulled up along the curb. The driver got out, pushed an old lady aside, and opened the car door. A famous celebrity stepped out. His hair was a mess, and he needed it fixed right away.

The celebrity walked into the salon, and the Farmer followed him inside. The celebrity sat down and snapped his fingers. The Farmer picked up the electric clippers and stared at them.

The Farmer spun the chair around and grabbed the celebrity.

The Farmer held him tight and got to work. *Bzzz! Bzzz! Bzzz!* The job was done in two seconds flat.

Everyone in the salon watched in horror. Who was this crazy man?

There was a high-pitched scream from the celebrity's driver, who threw himself onto the Farmer.

Chapter Four

BRIGHT LIGHTS, BIG CITY

The Farmer was in big trouble. Or

was he?

The celebrity stood up, saw

himself in the mirror, and . . . was

thrilled! His new haircut was perfect!

The man gave the Farmer a high

five. Everyone clapped.

The salon owner, Meryl, had found a new stylist.

The Farmer's haircuts were a hit. Photos of the celebrity's new look appeared all over the Internet. Suddenly everyone wanted the Farmer to do their hair, and the salon became very, very busy. The Farmer—now known as "Mr. X"—was famous!

Back at the farm, Shaun and the Flock were worried about the Farmer. They needed him.

The sheep traveled to the city to search for him. They dressed themselves in jackets, skirts, and scarves to look human. But where was the Farmer? Shaun had brought an old photo of the Farmer, which he used to create a "MISSING" poster.

However, the Farmer was not hard to find. He was on a giant bill-board right above them! The sign advertised Meryl's hair salon and its star stylist.

Bitzer, Shaun, and the rest of the sheep went to the salon. They saw the Farmer through the window. It was up to Shaun to march inside and get him.

When the Farmer saw Shaun, he did not remember him! To him, Shaun was just a strange sheep wandering the city. Bitzer came in to help Shaun, but another stylist at the salon grabbed a broom and pushed the two of them out.

They joined the rest of the Flock outside. It was no use. The Farmer did not remember any of them. This was a disaster! What could they do?

Chapter Five
THE RESCUE

When night fell, the sheep gathered under a bridge to keep warm and figure out what to do. Shaun had an idea: they would kidnap the Farmer and take him back to Mossy Bottom Farm.

The Flock returned to the salon. This time, they brought a gate.

They watched through the window as the Farmer, Meryl, and the rest of the staff cleaned up the salon after a long, busy day.

Knock, knock!

The humans all looked toward the window. They saw a sheep jump over a gate. Then another. And another. One by one, the people started counting, and then their eyelids closed and they all fell asleep. Two people's heads dropped forward into their ice-cream cones. A bus swerved as the driver fell asleep.

A salesman at Trampoline World slumped down . . . and bounced back up . . . and slumped down . . . and bounced back up.

The rescue sheep dragged the sleeping Farmer out of the salon. Time to get back to Mossy Bottom Farm!

The farmhouse at Mossy Bottom was a complete mess. There was food and garbage everywhere! The pigs had been very, very bad.

One of the pigs looked out the window and spotted the Farmer, who

was being dressed in his farm clothes
by the sheep.

Oh, no! The big pig party quickly
became a big pig clean-up. One pig
cleaned off a photo of the Farmer.

He had drawn a mustache on it! Another one did the dishes. As the last pig left in a hurry, he stopped and wiped off the door-knob to remove any prints.

The next day, the pigs had nothing to laugh at. The Farmer had his memory back and had returned to normal. The pigs were back in their pigsties. No more partying for them. They were not happy.

The Flock *was* happy. The Farmer
was home. Shaun was the happiest.
He had the most stylish hairdo
around!